To nicolos, Hailey and

enjoy all the animals
and the story
Ron Reid

the book's author

Hi guys :)

I forgot to include this in with
your 2008 Christmas — so —
how about Easter 2009 :)
Since you all are a little older —
maybe Nick or Hailey can
read this to Jen ?!!

grandma
Thompson....

# Templeton TURTLE

## Goes Exploring

Written by
Ron Pridmore

Illustrated by
Michele-lee Phelan

Templeton Turtle Goes Exploring
Published by Bridgeway Books
P.O. Box 80107
Austin, Texas 78758

For more information about our books, please write to us, call 512.478.2028, or visit our website at www.bridgewaybooks.net.

Library of Congress Control Number: 2007943903

ISBN-13: 978-1-934454-21-3
ISBN-10: 1-934454-21-4

Bridgeway
Books

10 9 8 7 6 5 4 3 2 1

*To my family for believing in me and supporting me.*

Templeton Turtle hatched today.

For the first time, he admired the beautiful, blue sky and enjoyed the warm sun shining on his shell. He was excited and curious about the world outside his egg.

Although Templeton didn't know much yet, he did know that his mother loved him more than anything.

Templeton wanted to start discovering new things, so he turned to his mother and asked, "May I please go exploring?"

"Yes, Templeton," she said with a gentle smile. "You can explore around the water's edge, but only if you promise to stay where I can see you. You are very young and small, and there is much you do not know about life outside your egg. I don't want anything to happen to you."

Templeton promised, "I will stay where you can see me," and humming softly to himself, he set off on his first big adventure.

As he walked to the edge of the pond, Templeton noticed an odd creature standing in the water. It had a long neck and a very long beak. It stood completely still and did not move, not even a little bit.

Templeton thought this was strange, so he swam out to where the creature stood and asked...

"What are you looking at?"

The creature scowled and said, "Young turtle, go home. You are scaring away the fish!"

But Templeton was still curious and ignored the tall creature's scowl. "What is your name, mister?" he asked.

In a gruff voice, the creature replied,
"My name is Mr. Blue." Then, with a loud
squawk, he spread his wings
and flew away.

Feeling a little sad,
Templeton shrugged.
"Oh well," he said,
and he continued on
his adventure.

As Templeton continued to explore, he wondered who he would meet next. "I hope they are friendlier than Mr. Blue," he said to himself.

Then, a long, skinny creature with pretty stripes on its skin came slithering by.

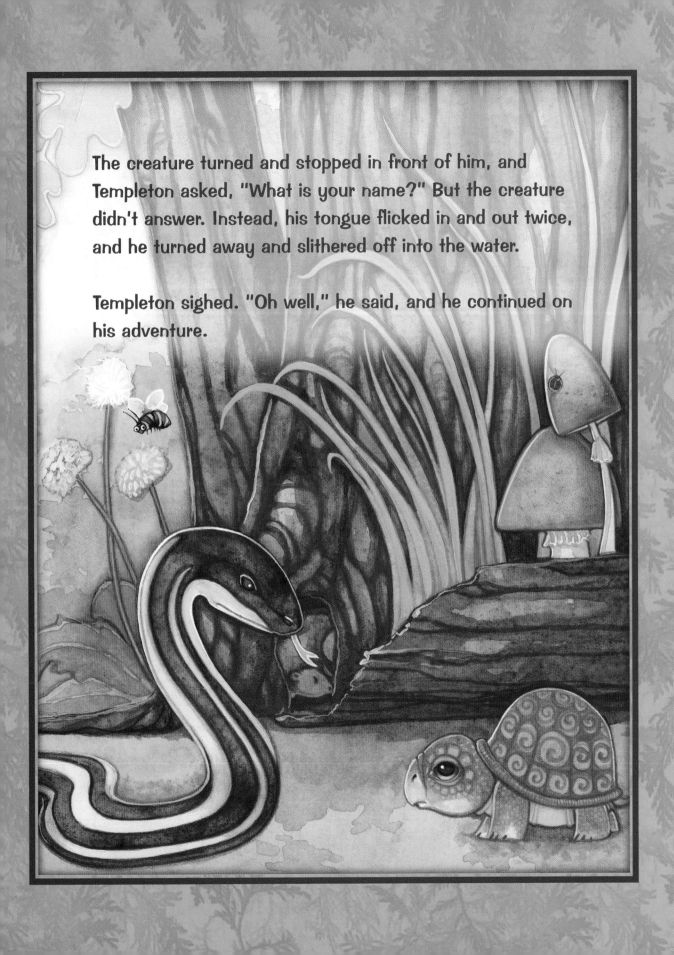

The creature turned and stopped in front of him, and Templeton asked, "What is your name?" But the creature didn't answer. Instead, his tongue flicked in and out twice, and he turned away and slithered off into the water.

Templeton sighed. "Oh well," he said, and he continued on his adventure.

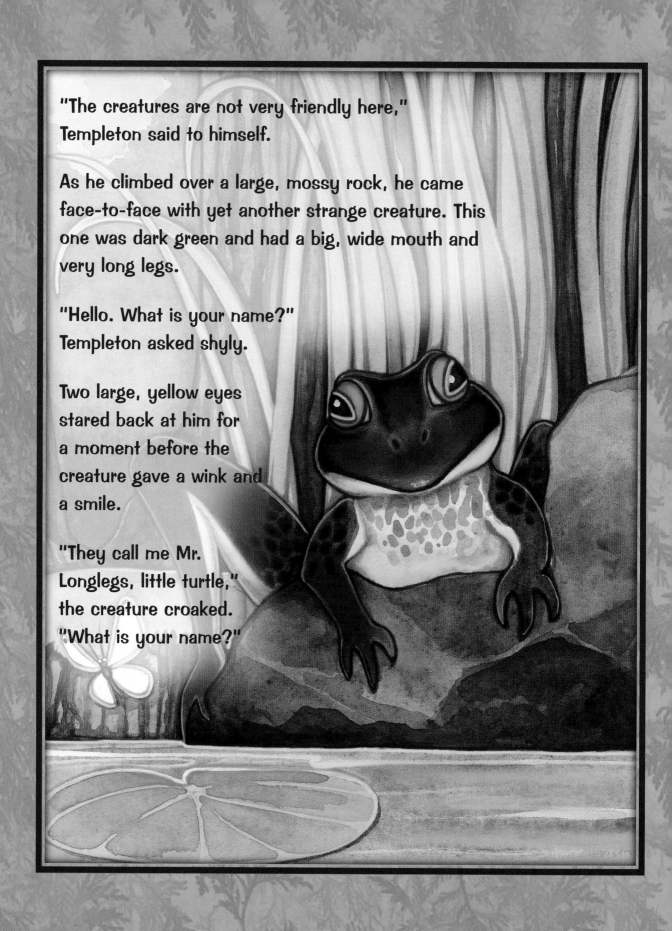

"The creatures are not very friendly here,"
Templeton said to himself.

As he climbed over a large, mossy rock, he came
face-to-face with yet another strange creature. This
one was dark green and had a big, wide mouth and
very long legs.

"Hello. What is your name?"
Templeton asked shyly.

Two large, yellow eyes
stared back at him for
a moment before the
creature gave a wink and
a smile.

"They call me Mr.
Longlegs, little turtle,"
the creature croaked.
"What is your name?"

Templeton was glad to finally meet a friend.
"My name is Templeton," he said.

Mr. Longlegs smiled and asked, "Would
you like to come for a swim?"

Templeton looked at the water and then at
his new friend. He wanted to go swimming,
but he also wanted to explore some more.
"No, thank you, but I will come and visit you again
tomorrow if that's okay."

Mr. Longlegs nodded cheerfully and jumped into the
water. Feeling happy, Templeton continued to explore.

All of a sudden, five curious creatures with grey and white fur, black masks on their faces, and little black paws tumbled down to the edge of the pond.

One was big and the others were small, but all were larger than Templeton. When they saw him, they began to chitter and chatter, and he felt a little scared.

The biggest creature sniffed him and looked at him with curious, black eyes.

Templeton was frightened and asked, "Who are you?"

"I am Mrs. Raccoon, little turtle. Your mother is my friend," she said kindly. "What are you doing so far from her side?"

"I am exploring," Templeton replied.

Mrs. Racoon chittered and chattered as she rubbed her front paws together. "There are many dangers here at the pond. Maybe you should go back to your mother where it is safe."

Thinking of all the creatures who had been unfriendly, Templeton agreed. "I am going home now," he said with a smile. "I have enjoyed my first adventure. Can I come and visit you tomorrow?"

Mrs. Racoon and her children smiled and nodded. "Good-bye, Templeton. We will see you tomorrow." After watching them leave, Templeton turned around and started walking back to where his mother waited.

Suddenly, there was a loud noise.

"What is that?" Templeton wondered aloud as the ground began to shake and the grass began to tremble.

Three large creatures, the largest he had ever seen, were running toward him. They looked mean and scary with big, long horns upon their heads, and they made strange mooing sounds.

They were so huge that they couldn't see Templeton hiding in the grass. "They are going to stomp on me!" he cried as he tucked his head and legs into his shell. "I want my mother!"

He could hear the creatures coming closer. The ground began to shake even harder, and he began to cry.

Templeton didn't want to be on his adventure anymore.

Suddenly, Templeton felt
something pick him up. He popped
his head out of his shell and
looked around.

He was flying!

Before he could turn and see who had rescued him, he was placed gently on the ground next to his mother. She was happy that her son was safe, and she hugged him close.

"What happened?" asked Templeton.

His mother softly replied, "Mr. Blue saved you."

"He did?" Templeton asked with wide eyes and a smile. "So he does like me?"

His mother smiled back and said,
"Of course he does. Whether we have fur,
feathers, flippers, wings, scales, or shells, we all
watch over each other down here by the pond."

Templeton felt very happy as he yawned and cuddled down into his bed of leaves. His first day out of the egg had been filled with adventure and new friends. He could not wait until tomorrow.

The End

# About the Author

While growing up in the country, Ron Pridmore always dreamed of writing a book about animals. He hopes his first book about brave Templeton will foster a fondness for animals among young audiences. Ron lives in Fairfield, California, with his wife, Maria, and son, Diego.

# About the Illustrator

Michele-lee Phelan wanted to be a professional artist since she was a girl. She is inspired by nature, including a few furry and feathered companions of her own. Michele-lee has painted the covers of several fantasy novels and is working toward completing her first art book. She and her family live at the base of the Blue Mountains in Australia.